My Daughter and Me

My Daughter and Me

A Devotional to Help Girls Pray and Perceive What Mama Used to Say

As is the Mother, so is her Daughter.
—Ezekiel 16:44 (KJV)

Yolanda Burroughs

Copyright © 2019 by Yolanda Burroughs.

Cover Design by Kenneth L. Keith, I

ISBN:	Softcover	978-1-7960-1796-0
	eBook	978-1-7960-1795-3

All rights reserved. No part of this book may be reproduced or transmitted in any form or by any means, electronic or mechanical, including photocopying, recording, or by any information storage and retrieval system, without permission in writing from the copyright owner.

Scripture quotations marked KJV are from the Holy Bible, King James Version (Authorized Version). First published in 1611. Quoted from the KJV Classic Reference Bible, Copyright © 1983 by The Zondervan Corporation.

Scripture quotations marked NIV are taken from the Holy Bible, New International Version®. NIV®. Copyright © 1973, 1978, 1984 by International Bible Society. Used by permission of Zondervan. All rights reserved. [Biblica]

Any people depicted in stock imagery provided by Getty Images are models, and such images are being used for illustrative purposes only.
Certain stock imagery © Getty Images.

Print information available on the last page.

Rev. date: 02/22/2019

To order additional copies of this book, contact:
Xlibris
1-888-795-4274
www.Xlibris.com
Orders@Xlibris.com
791742

CONTENTS

(In no particular order I have chronicled the words I recall that my mama used to say. My hope is that mothers, daughters, sisters, and girlfriends will read and share this insightful devotional to draw closer to God the Father and each other.)

Preface ix
Introduction xi

Segment 1: Exposed 1
Segment 2: Expound 19
Segment 3: Encourage 37
Segment 4: Examine 53
Segment 5: Expressed 71
Segment 6: Engaged 89
Segment 7: Excited 107
Segment 8: Evolve 119

Upcoming Books 139

For my mother,

Brenda Joyce Biggers

This devotional is dedicated to my mother, Brenda Joyce Biggers, who is the strongest, wisest, and most loving and considerate woman that has ever walked the earth, in my humble opinion. I am so thankful that God, in his infinite wisdom, chose to bless my siblings and I with a nurturing mother who loves us, taught us, disciplined us, and daily modeled goodness for us during our childhood. Even now, through her unrelenting and selfless love, she unconditionally loves us. She is more than just a parent. She is a wonderful friend, a splendiferous grandmother, and a stellar great-grandmother too.

After fifty years looking, learning, and striving to become at least half the woman I see in my mother, unabashedly I admit I now understand and really appreciate all the truthful words of wisdom "Mama used to say." I did not always understand her words in my youth, but now that I am much older and wiser, I am living her words and striving to help others do the same. So thank you. Thank you, Mother. For your walk, witness, and words of wisdom, I thank you. I love you so much more than words can adequately convey!

Also, to every woman God blessed to bear a child (or children) and particularly to the daughters who recognize the blessedness of being called daughter, I pray this devotional will cause you to smile at all the memories of saying and/or hearing the words *Mama used to say*. More importantly, it is my hope that you will maximize every moment you now have with your mother, daughters, girls, and ladies in your life. Allow the familiar words of a mother, and the faithful words of our Heavenly Father to lead you into a more intimate relationship with God and one another.

I thank God for every woman who is a daughter, and every daughter who is, and will become, a mother. There really is no greater love and no stronger earthly bond than the love and bond between *My Daughter & Me*! Happy reading, reminiscing, praying, and bonding.

Finally, I hope you do not ignore what is written, because mama use to say a hard head makes a soft behind.

Preface

Have you ever listened to the words your mother spoke and wondered, what does that mean? Clearly, the passion with which your mother spoke assured you she was fully aware of the message she was conveying, and she meant every single spoken word. However, you were in a fog. Clueless.

Well, if that was your experience, I assure you I, too, felt clueless countless times. Whenever (or perhaps I should say if ever) I was bold enough to ask the meaning of what was spoken, my mother would then adamantly exclaim other words that only added to the ambiguity. She would say words like, "You will understand it better by and by." Or "You will figure it out and thank me later."

Mama was right. Here I sit half a century old and writing book number three just to convey what my mother's words meant and still mean to me. Finally, I unequivocally can say: Mother, I think I got it! I think I understand the words of wisdom you imparted. In fact, I not only understand what "Mama used to say"; many of her words now I am guilty of repeating to others. Granted that a few of Mama's words had little biblically spiritual value, but even those words make a lot of natural common sense. Good spiritual and common sense are great commodities and a rarity nowadays.

Since Mama would say, "Good sense ain't common," this devotional is written to *expose* and *expound* upon the words my mother and countless other mothers have shared for many years. I also hope to *encourage* you to *examine* the word of God. May you allow our Heavenly Father's words to be "a lamp unto your feet and a light unto your pathway."

Yes, this devotional will expose, expound, encourage, and examine maternal and divine love as it is *expressed* through the written word of God and the words Mama spoke. Hopefully, after reading this devotional, you will *engage* in meaningful prayer and dialogue with your daughter and feel *excited* enough to share with other women and girls in your life. Together, mothers and daughters will *evolve*.

Introduction

Wait. Wait one minute. When did this happen? When did I become this grown woman? Seems like just yesterday I was sitting Indian style on my bed, thinking to myself, "I can't wait until I become a grown-up, to get out of this house, and make my own rules!" Well, maybe not yesterday, but certainly I remember thinking those thoughts as clearly as I am sitting here in the garage of my home, writing this journal. As an independent woman paying my own bills since moving out of my mother's house in my early twenties, I soon discovered life was much easier as a dependent youth living at home with my mother and siblings.

In fact, my childhood was so good and blessed, and my memories were so fond; to this very day, home is wherever my mother is. Do not misunderstand me. With the help and by the grace of God, I have a wonderful and blessed home in which I live with much joy and peace. However, there is something so very special about mothers. There is something special, extra special, about my mother. There is something divinely special about good mothers because mothers and motherhood are God's idea.

The sad reality is not every girl (or boy) has had the blessed privilege of growing up in a house with their mother. Some were in the house with their mother, but they cannot truthfully say they had a good mother. My heart aches for them. I pray for them. If you are one of them, I am praying for you!

This devotional is my gift back to God for his special gift to me. It is my hope that on the pages of this short devotional, girls may come to know and share the same wonderful joys I have been blessed to experience because I was raised by a good mother. I hope the good mothers will smile and remember their words to their daughters and be encouraged to know that just like me (and them), sooner or later their daughters will get the message.

I hope mothers and daughters who have not necessarily given God their best when it comes to the mother-and-daughter relationship will be encouraged by this devotional. I hope both mother and child will experience a fresh outlook on the maternal relationship God ordained. I hope both will come to understand and embrace the importance of this divine relationship and commit to enhancing and strengthening the bond for as long as God allows them.

Finally, I hope and pray that this devotional inspires both mother and daughter to look to our Heavenly Father for the love, guidance, strength, and support that everyone needs from a parent. After all, the Bible says, "Can a mother forget the baby at her breast and have no compassion on the child she has borne? Though she may forget, I [God] will not forget you!" (Isaiah 49:15, NIV).

Praise God for a Heavenly Father who will not only hear but will answer prayers. Pray. Pray independently. Pray domiciliary. Whenever, however, with whomever, and for whatever, this devotional is calling you to pray!

Segment 1: Exposed

Have nothing to do with the fruitless deeds of darkness, but rather expose them.

—Ephesians 5:11 (NIV)

The greatest and most fatal temptation to humankind is the temptation to disobey, deny, or ignore the truth. So many times during my childhood, although I presumed to know everything and thought I was rather wise, I knew far less than I wanted to admit, then and even now. But in his infinite wisdom, God knew what type of woman I would need in a mother. God knew I would need a person in my life to shape and nurture my strong character and personality without breaking my spirit.

My mother was, beyond all doubt, the right kind of nurturer. When I was too timid, she knew how to encourage me to find my strength. When I was too strong, stiff-necked, and unyielding, she knew how to temper and settle my bullish nature as well. Somehow my mother always knew the right words to speak even when I did not care to hear or heed her words.

Chapter 1, Expose It, contains the hard words Mama used to say to educate me. Sometimes her words about life, people, the world, and my character and potential, seemed hard and cruel, yet necessary. Today, Mama's words are the undeniable rules by which I choose to live my life. I pray the words my mama used to say will resonate, bless, and guide you too. I am most confident many of her words are the same words you have said or heard your mother say too!

Day 1

"Everybody Ain't Your Friend"

I was the child who wanted to get along with everybody. Countless times, Mama would say, "Everybody ain't your friend." Just because people smile at you does not mean they are your friend. She cautioned me not to use the word *friend* so lightly. She told me a friend is the person who has your best interest in mind and will not intentionally hurt you, lie to you, lead or tempt you to do anything that is wrong.

Let Us Pray: Lord, open our eyes so we can see what people are trying to hide from us. Help us hear even the words that are not spoken so that we are never fooled or deceived by people who say they are our friends. In Jesus's name I pray. Amen.

Let Us Learn the Spiritual Lesson: Jeremiah 17:5 (NIV) "This is what the LORD says: 'Cursed is the one who trusts in man, who draws strength from mere flesh and whose heart turns away from the LORD.'"

Let Us Reflect: What have you learned? What can you do better or differently now?

_____

_____

_____

Day 2

"Not Every Closed Eye Is Sleep"

Sometimes people play possum. They pretend to be asleep so they can hear and see something they do not believe you will say or do in their presence. Or it could be their way of ignoring you. People also fake actions because they have evil intentions. Be alert so you are not easily fooled.

Let Us Pray: Lord, keep me from speaking words I do not want others to hear and help me to refrain from actions I do not want others to see. Let my ways and words always please you and not offend others. Teach me to put my trust in you and protect me from anyone who may wish to do me harm. In Jesus's name I pray. Amen.

Let Us Learn the Spiritual Lesson: 2 Samuel 13:2, 14 (NIV) "Amnon became so obsessed with his sister Tamar that he made himself ill . . . and since he was stronger than she, he raped her."

Let Us Reflect: What have you learned? What can you do better or differently now?

_____

_____

_____

Day 3

"Never Burn the Bridge That Crossed You Over"

Mama used to say, "Never burn the bridge that crossed you over" to stress the importance of treating people right. Never forget to express gratitude for the good deeds and favors others granted you. Never mistreat the people who helped you or forget the kindness you were shown. Regard people and their good deeds in your heart and thank them.

Let Us Pray: Lord, with a sincere spirit of humility and thankfulness, I praise you and ask you to help me honor, remember, and bless the people who blessed me. Do not let me become my very own enemy. In Jesus's name I pray. Amen.

Let Us Learn the Spiritual Lesson: Zechariah 13:6 (KJV) "And one shall say unto him, What are these wounds in thine hands? Then he shall answer, Those with which I was wounded in the house of my friends."

Let Us Reflect: What have you learned? What can you do better or differently now?

_____
_____
_____
_____
_____
_____
_____

Day 4

"A Bird in the Hand Is Better Than Two in a Bush"

Mama wanted me to make wise decisions. She did not want me to risk the good things I already have while trying to get the things I wanted but did not need or could not afford. Ambition and risk-taking are not wrong. Mama simply cautioned me to consider the pros and cons of all things before jumping in.

Let Us Pray: Lord, teach me to be grateful for the things I possess and enjoy. Help me to be content with what you have already given me and grant me discernment and wisdom so that every decision I make is in alignment with your purpose. As I walk by faith, help me keep all things in the right perspective. In Jesus's name I pray. Amen.

Let Us Learn the Spiritual Lesson: **1 Timothy 6:7–8 (KJV)** "For we brought nothing into this world, and it is certain we can carry nothing out. And having food and raiment let us be therewith content."

Let Us Reflect: What have you learned? What can you do better or differently now?

_____

_____

Day 5

"Don't Ever Bite the Hand That Feeds You"

After getting caught taking change from my mother's purse to buy candy without asking, she whipped me and said, "Don't ever bite the hand that feeds you." Mama wanted me to understand how foolish it is to steal from the person who gives to you. Stealing is wrong, period. But what she was specifically teaching me is that it is most foolish to steal from the person who is helping you. By hurting them, you hurt yourself.

Let Us Pray: Lord, I know stealing is wrong. Help me to always do that which is right and honest. Teach me to work hard to earn the things I desire and never take anything without asking, especially from those you send to bless and help me. In Jesus's name I pray. Amen.

Let Us Learn the Spiritual Lesson: Deut. 8: 10–11a (KJV) "When you have eaten and are satisfied, praise the LORD your God for the good land he has given you. Be careful that you do not forget the LORD your God."

Let Us Reflect: What have you learned? What can you do better or differently now?

_____

_____

Day 6

"Watch Your Mouth, God Will Make You Eat Your Words"

Honestly, I am not sure if my mother spoke these words to me when I was a youth, but I cannot count the times she had emphatically spoken them to me as an adult. Beyond a doubt, she reminds me that God will judge the words I speak. A lot of bad weight has come from eating words from my mouth that I did not want to eat.

Let Us Pray: Heavenly Father, your words are truth. They are powerful and purposeful. Teach me to speak your word like Jesus, so I only speak words that I would want to eat.

Let Us Learn the Spiritual Lesson: 2 Kings 7:19 (NIV)
"The officer had said to the man of God, 'Look, even if the LORD should open the floodgates of the heavens, could this happen?' The man of God had replied, 'You will see it with your own eyes, but you will not eat any of it!'"

Let Us Reflect: What have you learned? What can you do better or differently now?

_____

_____

Day 7

"If You Lie, You Will Steal, If You Steal, You Will Kill"

I do not know which incident caused the most pain, taking change from my mother's purse without asking or the whipping she gave me after lying about taking the money. My mother did not put up with lies, period. To get caught telling a lie was absolutely the worst and most unacceptable of all my childhood offenses. She believed lying led to greater sins and eventually yielded undesirable results.

Let Us Pray: Jesus, thank you for plainly showing me the importance of always speaking the truth. Teach me the dangers of giving Satan access into my life with lies. Teach me to speak, regard, and honor truth, always.

Let Us Learn the Spiritual Lesson: Acts 5:3–4 (NIV)
"Peter asked, 'Ananias, how is it that Satan has so filled your heart that you have lied to the Holy Spirit . . . What made you think of doing such a thing? You have not lied just to human beings but to God.'"

Let Us Reflect: What have you learned? What can you do better or differently now?

_____
_____
_____
_____
_____
_____
_____

Day 8

"What Doesn't Come Out in the Wash Will Show Up in the Rinse"

It was a bright, sunny, and hot day. My siblings and I were playing outside. I clearly recall my brother asking to ride my bike around the square pavement just outside our apartment. Of course, I said yes. I heard the Popsicle truck coming around and wanted to catch him before he left the complex. So I yelled for my brother to hurry and bring my bike. Each time he came close, he pretended to slow down only to speed up and passed by me again and again. He made me miss the Popsicle truck, and I angrily screamed out a bad four-letter word. My mother heard us fussing and called us into the house and asked who cussed. I was always terrified of whippings, so I lied and said, "Not me, Mama. It was him." My brother truthfully denied using the cuss word my mother knew she heard one of us holler out.

My mother sat on a big red chair and had my brother and I both sit on the floor in front of her. She reminded us that it was always better to tell the truth. Each time she asked, "Who cussed?" I denied cussing and so did my brother. Each time she whipped us with the belt and said, "Sooner or later somebody will tell me the truth. What doesn't come out in the wash will show up in the rinse."

Eventually, my brother took the blame for me and was punished on top of the long belt whippings we had already suffered that Saturday afternoon. After years of carrying the mental guilt and out of love for my brother for covering my wrong, I finally told my mother the truth. Thus, proving what Mama used to say—"what does not come out in the wash will come out in the rinse."

Let Us Pray: Heavenly Father, thank you for extending to us the ultimate sacrifice for my sins by sending Jesus to die on the cross in my place. Even though he was innocent of any guilt, he willingly died for me and for the sins of the whole world. Please forgive me for the times I have not willingly and honestly confessed my sins and faults. Starting today, please help me to be quick to confess and admit my wrongs to you and those who I might hurt or offend in the future. Thank you for being a forgiving God who answers when I pray. Amen.

Let Us Learn the Spiritual Lesson: Genesis 38:25 (NIV)
"As she was being brought out, she sent a message to her father-in-law. 'I am pregnant by the man who owns these,' she said. And she added, 'See if you recognize whose seal and cord and staff these are.'"

Let Us Reflect: What have you learned? What can you do better or differently now?

_____
_____
_____
_____
_____
_____

Segment 2: Expound

*Wisdom is the principal thing; therefore, get wisdom:
and with all thy getting get understanding.*
—Proverbs 4:7 (KJV)

The words "went over my head" is an idiomatic expression that is most evocative of how I felt many times when my mother sternly spewed her motherly advice, commands, or reprimands. Nevertheless, she was resolute to share wisdom and truth, as well as to answer the countless questions I asked in search of understanding.

Segment 2, Expound, are the words Mama used to say to explain deeper things to me; things I would not and could not learn in a classroom. Only as a loving parent would, my mother tried to explain the complex truths about life and people that were beyond my experience and mental comprehension. Oft times, despite her patient and purposeful mother-and-daughter talks, I was still left wondering, "What?" I resigned to pretend like I understood so I could quickly get back to whatever I was doing before I was trapped in my mother's teachings.

I thank God the ambiguity was arrested by life's experiences. The light switch came on, and now I am experiencing complete liberty in the vast areas of which my mother spoke. I pray these shared nuggets of motherly wisdom will do the same for you.

Day 9

"An Empty Wagon Makes the Most Noise"

The person who first spoke these words to me was not my mother. She was my fifth-grade teacher at the elementary school I attended. She was the fifth-grade teacher that every mother would love, a mother-away-from-home type of teacher. Ugh! I cannot forget her. Her frequent, nearly day-by-day parent-teacher conference calls to my mother about my misbehavior were one of my greatest stressors as a child. She told me to turn around in my chair and stop talking. I followed her instructions, but before the class ended, I was caught in the same position running my mouth again. Finally, she blurted out, "Ms. Burroughs, an empty wagon makes the most noise."

By the time I got home from school that day, my mother had a belt in her hand. After several lashes, she repeated, "So an empty wagon makes the most noise, shut your mouth. Don't cry now." After I calmed down, my mother explained she sent me to school to learn and not to play and run my mouth. It was no wonder why my math grades were substandard. My mother stressed the importance of closing my mouth and opening my ears. She explained there is a time and place for everything. During classroom instructions, talking and playing were not for that time or the place.

Let Us Pray: Lord, your word declares there is a proper time and place for everything. Help me to understand, respect, and do what is right and proper during the right time and in the right place. When my attitude, words, and actions are out of alignment, like the handle on a wagon, please tug on the strings of my heart and pull me in the right direction. I pray in Jesus's name. Amen.

Let Us Learn the Spiritual Lesson: Ecclesiastes 3:1, 7, 11 (KJV) "To everything there is a season, and a time to every purpose under the heaven: . . . a time to keep silence, and a time to speak; . . . He hath made everything beautiful in his time: also he hath set the world in their heart, so that no man can find out the work that God maketh from the beginning to the end."

Let Us Reflect: What have you learned? What can you do better or differently now?

_____
_____
_____
_____
_____
_____
_____

Day 10

"A Dog That Brings a Bone, Carries a Bone"

My mother respected my privacy, but when she happened to hear or see anything out of order, she was quick to correct me. Just when my conversation was getting good and juicy, my mother would stand in my bedroom door and demand that I get off the phone. I was talking on the phone about the latest gossip around the school halls. My mother overheard my conversation, and she corrected me. Mama said, "A dog that brings a bone, carries a bone." She wanted me to understand that anyone who was quick to talk about other people and share secrets and someone else's business would do the very same thing to me. Gossip was wrong then, and gossip is wrong now. My mother's words about gossip seemed too harsh, but they helped me avoid a lot of mess as a young girl and as an adult woman.

Let Us Pray: Lord, you want me to speak words that edify and not condemn others. You want me to speak truth in love. Your word also instructs me to take care of my own business and refrain from being a busybody in the business of others. Forgive me for the times I have failed to obey your word in this area. If my words have caused any confusion or hurt to others, please grant me mercy and the opportunity to correct my wrongs. From this time forward, help me to be a loyal friend who respects the confidentiality of others.

Let Us Learn the Spiritual Lesson: Proverbs 11:13 (NIV)
"A gossip betrays a confidence, but a trustworthy person keeps a secret."

Let Us Reflect: What have you learned? What can you do better or differently now?

_____
_____
_____
_____
_____
_____
_____

Day 11

"Believe Nothing You Hear and Only One Half of What You See"

My mother quoted Edgar Allen Poe's words as if they were her own. I cannot recall when I first heard her say, "Believe nothing you hear, and only one half that you see," but she most diffidently drilled the words in my mind. Mama was cautioning me to check things out, to get the facts before running with the first thing I heard and saw. She tried to protect me from being impulsive.

Let Us Pray: Lord, teach me patience and diligence. Help me to seek you for insight and full understanding in all things. Give me keen discernment and keep me from making rash decisions based upon surface and carnal things. In Jesus's name I pray. Amen.

Let Us Learn the Spiritual Lesson: Mark 8:23–25 (NIV)
"He took the blind man by the hand and led him outside the village. When he had spit on the man's eyes and put his hands on him, Jesus asked, 'Do you see anything?' He looked up and said, 'I see people; they look like trees walking around.' Once more Jesus put his hands on the man's eyes. Then his eyes were opened, his sight was restored, and he saw everything clearly."

Let Us Reflect: What have you learned? What can you do better or differently now?

_____
_____
_____
_____
_____
_____
_____

Day 12

"Don't Let Your Left Hand Know What Your Right Hand Is Doing"

Mama said, "Don't let your left hand know what your right hands is doing" to teach me about doing the right thing without looking for praise from people. As the middle child, I was trying to find my place, my *niche*, the thing I could do better than my brother and sister. In my quest for self-worth and self-identity, I did things just to hear someone say "good job." Even if no one sees or comments on my good works, doing good is what I was taught to do.

Let Us Pray: Heavenly Father, just as Jesus went about doing good and not looking to hear praise from people, help me to do the same. In Jesus's name I pray. Amen.

Let Us Learn the Spiritual Lesson: Matthew 6:3–4 (NIV) "But when you give to the needy, do not let your left hand know what your right hand is doing, so that your giving may be in secret. Then your Father, who sees what is done in secret, will reward you."

Let Us Reflect: What have you learned? What can you do better or differently now?

Day 13

"You Got to Work Hard for What You Want"

"Anything Worth Having Is Worth Working For"

I was the new girl on the squad, but I cannot forget how badly I wanted to be the co-captain of my senior high school flagette squad. The tryouts included choreographing a dance and teaching it to others. I had two problems: I was not a good dancer, and I had never made up a dance routine. My mama said, "You got to work hard for what you want. Anything worth having is worth working for. I know you can do it, but what do you think?" I did it. I worked hard and won the main captain spot.

Let Us Pray: Lord, teach me to have faith in you and faith in myself too. As I dream, give me the strength and mind to also work to make my dreams become a reality. I pray this by faith and with thanksgiving in Jesus's name. Amen.

Let Us Learn the Spiritual Lesson: Genesis 29:20 (KJV)
"And Jacob served seven years for Rachel; and they seemed unto him but a few days, for the love he had to her."

Let Us Reflect: What have you learned? What can you do better or differently now?

_____
_____
_____
_____
_____
_____
_____

Day 14

"If You Want to Stop Going in Circles, Quit Cutting Corners"

Growing up in a single-parent home, my mother made certain that we knew how to take care of ourselves, but also that we helped to carry the weight of taking care of our home. Household chores were mandatory not optional. Of all the chores, washing and ironing clothes were the ones I literally despised and often tried to avoid. I would half iron the clothes, improperly fold them, and hang them across the hangers any kind of way. Many times, she removed my clothes from my dresser drawers, off the hangers, and she tossed them on my bed. Then Mama would say, "If you want to stop going in circles, quite cutting corners." She said, "Do it right the first time and you won't have to do it again."

Let Us Pray: Lord, help me to do everything I do to the best of my ability. In Jesus's name I pray. Amen.

Let Us Learn the Spiritual Lesson: Mark 7:37 (NIV)
"He has done everything well," they said. "He even makes the deaf hear and the mute speak."

Let Us Reflect: What have you learned? What can you do better or differently now?

_____
_____
_____
_____
_____
_____
_____

Day 15

"If It Looks Like a Duck, Swims Like a Duck, Quacks Like a Duck, It Is Probably a Duck"

I cannot tell you how many times I tried to wear makeup and dress like a grown-up lady while in elementary school. I do vividly recall sneaking out of the house wearing makeup. I was standing at the bus stop thinking I had gotten away, but before my school bus came, my brother walked by and saw me. He wiped my face with his hand. The makeup that did not come off was now smeared all over my face. My brother then yelled, "You are not grown. I am going to tell Mama."

Later that day, my mother explained that I was much too young to wear makeup. Mama said, "If it looks like a duck, swims like a duck, quacks like a duck, it is probably a duck." My mama wanted me to understand that people would assume things about me based upon my appearance. It was my responsibility as a young girl to look, dress, and carry myself like a young girl. Then and now, the way a person dresses and carry themselves will strongly affect how they are perceived by others.

Let Us Pray: Lord, help me to present myself in a way that will bring glory and honor to your name and cause others to respect and properly treat me. I pray this prayer by faith and with thanksgiving. In Jesus's name. Amen.

Let Us Learn the Spiritual Lesson: Romans 12:1 (NIV)
"Therefore, I urge you, brothers and sisters, in view of God's mercy, to offer your bodies as a living sacrifice, holy and pleasing to God—this is your true and proper worship."

Let Us Reflect: What have you learned? What can you do better or differently now?

_____
_____
_____
_____
_____
_____
_____

Day 16

"You Will Appreciate This Later"

My mother raised me with a soft heart but an iron hand. She was quick to whip me back in line whenever I did not follow instructions or obey a rule. My mother was clear in her instructions, and she made sure I understood what was expected of me. So when a rule was broken, I could expect to receive correction. My mother would often say to me before, during, or after I was whipped by a belt and left crying and wiping tears from my face, "You will appreciate this later." Believe me when I say, I was always praying later would come sooner. For the life of me, I could not then see what I now know for sure! Discipline helps.

Let Us Pray: Lord, you always give a word of instruction and warning before you give punishment. Please help me understand that I should trust and obey you now, so that I can avoid unnecessary pain and sadness later. In Jesus's name. Amen.

Let Us Learn the Spiritual Lesson: Proverbs 13:24 (NIV)
"Whoever spares the rod hates their children, but the one who loves their children is careful to discipline them."

Let Us Reflect: What have you learned? What can you do better or differently now?

_____
_____
_____
_____
_____
_____
_____

Segment 3: Encourage

Listen, my son [daughter], to your father's instruction and do not forsake your mother's teaching. They are a garland to grace your head and a chain to adorn your neck.

—Proverbs 1:8–9 (NIV)

Encourage means "to give support and advice to (someone) so that they will do or continue to do something." My mother was the very first person to encourage me. She is perhaps my greatest source of encouragement as an adult. Time would not allow nor are words adequate to tell just how many times my mother's words of encouragement have helped me through the scariest, hardest, and most complex periods of my life as a child and as an adult. Both verbal and nonverbally, my mother has encouraged me.

From signing me up for sports teams, social organizations, and varied activities that I had no interest to be a part of, to sitting in the hot sun at football games and long parades, watching me march and perform in the band, my mother has always made her presence and support known. I was strongly encouraged to be a part of the Brownies and Girl Scouts, to cake decorating, sewing, tap, modern, and jazz dances, and swimming classes. Volleyball, basketball, tennis, and modeling lessons, followed by piano, clarinet, flute, and bass clarinet musical lessons filled my extracurricular calendar too. Intentionally and sacrificially, my mother did what every little girl needed. She encouraged me. You and every girl and woman you know also needs encouragement.

Day 17

"Always Do Your Best"

Sometimes I was awkward. Sometimes I was too timid and afraid. Sometimes I lacked confidence. Sometimes I simply did not have the will or drive to carry out the task at hand. Sometimes, I did not have the talent or skill set to do what was being asked, but it never mattered. None of it ever mattered as much as hearing my mama say, "Baby, always do your best."

She would always encourage me and sometimes sternly command me, "Always do your best." After which, Mama used to say, "When you do your best, that is all you can do." My mother's words were very wise words, I tell you. Her words were also very liberating. Once I did my best, I felt a sense of relief without guilt.

Even as an adult, I strive to live by those words, "Always do your best." I find rest in those words too!

Let Us Pray: Lord, I look to you to help me give and do my best in everything I do so that you are glorified. You made me how you want me. You gave me the gifts, talents, and abilities that I have. As I strengthen them and do my best, I know you will do the rest. Thank you!

Let Us Learn the Spiritual Lesson: Colossians 3:23–24 (NIV) "Whatever you do, work at it with all your heart, as working for the LORD, not for human masters, since you know that you will receive an inheritance from the LORD as a reward. It is the LORD Christ you are serving."

Let Us Reflect: What have you learned? What can you do better or differently now?

_____

_____

_____

_____

_____

_____

_____

Day 18

"Say Please and Thank You"

Mama use to say, "Say please and thank you." Candy was withheld and not so sweet spankings were given whenever I failed or refused to speak those words. As I matured and grew older, I discovered those invaluable couple of words would do exactly what Mama said they would. Mama always encouraged and demanded that I say please and thank you. She said, "Those words will take you far in life." Mama was right!

If you receive anything and want something more, saying please and thank you will deliver results that will open the door to much more than you can imagine and sometimes more than what is deserved. I am a witness.

Let Us Pray: Heavenly Father, you are the giver of every good and perfect gift. When I receive from others, help me to see that you are the person behind my blessings. Forgive me for the times I haven't said please or voiced my gratitude by saying thank you. Thank you for teaching me and giving me chances to put good lessons into practice. I begin my new way of thinking by saying thank you for all you have done for me. Please continue to help and bless me according to your will. In Jesus's name I pray. Amen.

Let Us Learn the Spiritual Lesson: Luke 17:15–19 (NIV) "One of them, when he saw he was healed, came back, praising God in a loud voice. He threw himself at Jesus' feet and thanked him—and he was a Samaritan. Jesus asked, "Were not all ten cleansed? Where are the other nine? Has no one returned to give praise to God except this foreigner?" Then he said to him, "Rise and go; your faith has made you well."

Let Us Reflect: What have you learned? What can you do better or differently now?

Day 19

"Saying I'm Sorry Does not Make You Weak"

Who likes to be wrong? Who wants to lose? A hard lesson to learn is that in this life, sometimes you win and sometimes you lose. There will be times when you are right and at other times, you will be wrong. When those times come, you may not always like how you feel, but you will be better off when you learn to say "I'm sorry" for whatever part you played. I hated to be wrong and to lose, but when Mama said, "Saying I'm sorry does not make you weak," I felt strong when I said them. You will too.

Let Us Pray: Heavenly Father, when I am wrong, help me to admit it and quickly say I'm sorry to whomever I owe an apology. Thank you for encouraging me to confess my sins so that you can freely bless me. In Jesus's name. Amen.

Let Us Learn the Spiritual Lesson: James 5:16 (NIV)
"Therefore confess your sins to each other and pray for each other so that you may be healed. The prayer of a righteous person is powerful and effective."

Let Us Reflect: What have you learned? What can you do better or differently now?

_____
_____
_____
_____
_____
_____
_____

Day 20

"Every Tub Sits on Its Own Bottom"

Growing up to become a responsible adult was not a choice. It was obligatory, sometimes painfully mandatory. My mother taught me the importance of being responsible and she meant the rules she laid down. Her rules guided and groomed me, and her discipline matured me. Whenever I questioned the reason why she was so hard on me, Mama would say, "Every tub sits on its own bottom" and "You got to learn to stand on your own two feet." Her encouragement often came with so many other terse truths and proverbs that I did not always understand until much later.

Let Us Pray: Lord, your word is truth, and I know you are teaching and guiding and growing me with your word. Help me to understand the importance of growing more mature in my walk with you. In Jesus's name I pray. Amen.

Let Us Learn the Spiritual Lesson: 1 Corinthians 14:20 (KJV) Good Children Thought Spiritual Immaturity Growth Adult Children Malice Thinking Aright Nurture Vengeance Children, attitudes towards Like Children Spirituality Manliness Childlikeness Babies Used As A Spiritual Image Spiritual Maturity Babies, Figurative Use Maturity, Sprritual "Brethren, be not children in understanding: howbeit in malice be ye children, but in understanding be men."

Let Us Reflect: What have you learned? What can you do better or differently now?

_____
_____
_____
_____
_____
_____
_____

Day 21

"Always Carry Yourself Like a Lady"

I went through this brief tomboy stage. I enjoyed playing marbles and peg (a game where you flipped a knife in the mud hoping it would land upright) with my brother. Whenever I was caught playing "boy games," my mama used to say, "Always carry yourself like a lady." She would explain why it was improper for young girls to do certain things like playing marbles with gapped opened legs while wearing a dress or skirt. Funny, but true. I dressed like a little girl even when I was playing rough like the boys.

Let Us Pray: Heavenly Father, thank you for creating in me a beautiful female. As I continue to mature, help me to know what is proper for females and resist anything that taints that image. I pray in Jesus's name. Amen.

Let Us Learn the Spiritual Lesson: Psalm 139:13–14 (The Living Bible??) "You made all the delicate, inner parts of my body and knit me together in my mother's womb. Thank you for making me so wonderfully complex! Your workmanship is marvelous—how well I know it."

Let Us Reflect: What have you learned? What can you do better or differently now?

_____
_____
_____
_____
_____
_____
_____

Day 22

"Respect Your Elders"

R E S P E C T. The late great Queen of Soul, Aretha Franklin sang, "What you want, baby, I got it. What you need, do you know I got it? All I'm asking is for a little respect when you get home." Aretha asked for it. My mama demanded it. My mama used to say, "Respect your elders," and she meant it. That meant listening to them, even if they were wrong without giving them word for word, which my mother called "back talk." Being patient, kind, and helpful to elders was expected of me. I was taught to respect myself and others, all others, but especially my elders.

Let Us Pray: Heavenly Father, your word tells me to respect the elderly. Help me to properly speak and act respectfully with my elders, especially as I get older. As I obey your word in this regard, I pray you also will bless me with a good long life. In Jesus's name I pray. Amen.

Let Us Learn the Spiritual Lesson: Leviticus 19:32 (NIV)
"Stand up in the presence of the aged, show respect for the elderly and revere your God. I am the LORD."

Let Us Reflect: What have you learned? What can you do better differently now?

_____
_____
_____
_____
_____
_____
_____

Day 23

"Whatever You Do Reflects Who You Are"

Lord Jesus, how many whippings did I get for half doing chores around the house? Too many to count, that is for sure. My mother was not anal, but she was surely a perfectionist in everything I ever saw her do. She demanded the same of me and would often say, "If I find one more thing you have half done, I am whipping your butt, and you are going to do it right. Whatever you do reflects who you are."

Let Us Pray: Heavenly Father, you are a God of excellence and your word says you do all things well. In whatever I do, please help me to do it in a manner that will properly reflect you and the person I daily strive to be. In Jesus's name I pray. Amen.

Let Us Learn the Spiritual Lesson: Colossians 3:23 (KJV) "And whatsoever ye do, do it heartily, as to the LORD, and not unto men;"

Let Us Reflect: What have you learned? What can you do better or differently now?

_____
_____
_____

Segment 4: Examine

Examine yourselves to see whether you are in the faith; test yourselves. Do you not realize that Christ Jesus is in you—unless, of course, you fail the test?
—2 Corinthians 13:5 (NIV)

I must admit, I have this great disdain for visiting the doctor's office. Although I am wise enough to know God gives doctors knowledge and wisdom to help enhance, preserve, and promote good health for my physical body, I am often guilty of delaying my physical checkups, particularly, the well-woman's exam. The well-woman's exam, also called gynecological, pelvic, and annual exams, are all about you, your body, and your reproductive health.

From about the age of thirteen, the doctor examines the body and checks the female's height, weight, and blood pressure. The doctor discusses the menstrual cycle, and anything and everything that concerns the female about her body and even her emotional health. The exams are necessary. The exams and doctor's visits are invasive but necessary. Yes, the exams can be uncomfortable and embarrassing, but the exams are necessary, just like many words Mama used to say and the conversations she forced us to have. This section includes some words Mama spoke that caused me to feel uncomfortable, but I am unquestionably super thankful she spoke them, and she made me listen.

Day 24

"Whatever You Do in the Dark Will Come to the Light"

I won't ever forget the day. I was sitting in my home economics class in twelfth grade when I looked across the table at the boy who was voted "Most Handsome Senior Boy" and I wanted to hook up with him! (Since I was voted "Most Beautiful Senior Girl," it just seemed right that the two of us would be a cute couple. Fortunately, I was much too shy to let him know I was attracted to him then and God forbids a female classmate might read this devotional and share my almost thirty-five-year-old secret now! Yikes!)

In my purse was a pack of birth control pills that I refused to take although my mother had taken my sister and I to the doctor for the prescription. I left my purse open with the pills visible on purpose, hoping this high school crush would see the pills and think I was one of the girls he could hook up with, and we would be protected. Just as I wanted, he saw the pills and said, "Hey now, Yolanda. I see you. I see you." Those were the exact and only words he said to me. I was so disappointed, but whenever I thought I could just take the pills and do it because I was safe, I would hear my mama's words. Mama said, "I am not giving you these pills so you can do it. I want you to wait. I want you to talk to me, and as your mother I want you to be safe. Do not be sneaky because whatever you do in the dark will come to the light."

55

Thank God I prayed and asked the Lord to help me keep my body. I never took the pills and never got another prescription. I truly believe God not only wants me to walk in the light, he helps me to avoid the works of darkness, and when I fall in other areas, he helps me still. Let him do the same for you!

Let Us Pray: Heavenly Father, Jesus said, "Men love darkness rather than light," and I know that is true in my life. Today, help me to think differently so that I love the light and the things that you love and the things that please you. Forgive me when I walk in darkness and always guide me back into the light of your love. In Jesus's name I pray. Amen.

Let Us Learn the Spiritual Lesson: Luke 8:17 (NIV)
"For there is nothing hidden that will not be disclosed, and nothing concealed that will not be known or brought out into the open."

Let Us Reflect: What have you learned? What can you do better or differently now?

_____
_____
_____
_____
_____
_____
_____

Day 25

"Keep People Out of Your Business and Don't Get Caught Up in Anybody Else's Mess

I rushed home from school and could not wait to cry on my mother's shoulder about the bad news of the day. I told one of my middle-school friends that a fellow classmate said he liked me. He liked me, but he had a girlfriend that everyone knew about. I begged my friend not to tell anyone. My exact words were, "I don't like him or his ugly girlfriend. I wish he stops talking to me." I told one friend, but before the last bell rang ending the school day, another person who rode the same school bus told the girl, "Yolanda said she hates you, and she wants to fight you and take your boyfriend." To make a long story short, I was almost forced into a fist fight at the school bus stop. I didn't like the girl or her boyfriend, but I didn't want to fight. I also didn't understand how all the mess started in the first place. At least, I didn't understand until I told my mother. My mother sternly said (among many other things), "Keep people out of your business and don't get caught up in anybody else's mess." I almost learned that lesson the hard way but thank God I did. Never tell one person something you will not mind anybody else knowing. Why? Because your friend talks to someone else besides you. Hopefully, you have loyal friends who will not betray your trust, but trust when I say it is your responsibility to protect yourself and your secrets. However, you should always strive to be the person who will respect and keep secrets others might share with you and stay away from mess! Mess stinks!

Let Us Pray: Heavenly Father, help me to trust you with every detail of my life and keep my mind focused on what you are doing in my life and on what you will have me to do. Lead me to pray for others and not concern myself with matters that will draw me away from doing that which pleases you. I pray in Jesus's name. Amen.

Let Us Learn the Spiritual Lesson: Proverbs 26:17 (NKJV)
"He who passes by and meddles in a quarrel not his own is like one who takes a dog by the ears."

1 Peter 4:15 (KJV) "But let none of you suffer as a murderer, or as a thief, or as an evildoer, or as a busybody in other men's matters"

Let Us Reflect: What have you learned? What can you do better or differently now?

_____
_____
_____
_____
_____
_____

Day 26

"Show Me Your Friends and I Will Show You Your Future"

My middle-school friends were super cool and fun to be around, but we got into a lot of trouble, often. Almost weekly, I found myself in the principal's office during the day. I can also remember crying myself to sleep on the evenings when my mother whipped my butt from the teacher/parent phone calls that almost always followed my mischievous behavior. Some days I didn't know which was worse, the whippings or the long lectures. Mama would say, "Show me your friends and I will show you your future . . . hanging out with the wrong people will get you nowhere you want to go, unless you want to end up in jail or an early grave." I have lived long enough to see a few people I once called friends end up in both places.

Let Us Pray: Lord, give me the wisdom to choose my friends wisely so that my walk and witness are protected, and my ways are pleasing to you. I ask this in faith, according to your will. In Jesus's name. Amen.

Let Us Learn the Spiritual Lesson: 1 Corinthians 15:33 (NIV) "Do not be misled: 'Bad company corrupts good character.'"

Let Us Reflect: What have you learned? What can you do better or differently now?

_____
_____
_____
_____
_____
_____
_____

Day 27

"Keep Your Mind Open and Legs Closed"

I cannot tell you how many people are astonished when I share my testimony that I am a fifty-year-old virgin. I have *never* engaged in sexual intercourse not only because I firmly believe God's word concerning my body being the temple of the Holy Ghost, but also because I was afraid of disappointing my mother. From childhood until my early adulthood whenever I came close to falling to my lustful desires, subconsciously I would hear my mother's words saying, "Girl, keep your mind open and your legs closed. Get an education and leave those babies where they are. You have plenty time to be grown."

Now, I am fully grown and have absolutely no regrets about keeping my legs closed not because Mama said so, but because God's standards are still right, and holiness is still the way! Love yourself enough to save your body for the man that will be a faithful husband to you. Free yourself of the needless worries of contracting STDs, heartbreak from relationship breakups, having babies outside of marriage, and the embarrassment of getting a bad reputation from sexual partners who will be all too glad to share their experience with you with others. You deserve better. In fact, you deserve the best! Save yourself!

Let Us Pray: Lord, thank you for your godly standards that are designed to safeguard my body and mind and ensure that I can enjoy a good, wholesome life. Let your words forever ring in my head and teach me to adopt your moral standards as my own. In Jesus's name I pray. Amen.

Let Us Learn the Spiritual Lesson: 2 Corinthians 11:2, (KJV) "For I am jealous over you with godly jealousy: for I have espoused you to one husband, that I may present you as a chaste virgin to Christ."

Let Us Reflect: What have you learned? What can you do better or differently now?

_____
_____
_____
_____
_____
_____
_____

Day 28

"This Is Going to Hurt Me More Than It Hurts You"

My mother did not like to punish us. Her punishments were always a result of our disobedience to her rules. I was often warned and given more time and chances to correct my actions before I was punished. Even when I was being punished, she demonstrated and expressed her love. Before or while she was whipping me with a belt, I would hear Mama say, "This is going to hurt me more than it hurts you." Of course, I did not understand those words at the time, but today I am thankful for every time she loved me enough to correct and punish my misbehavior. It was for my good.

Let Us Pray: Lord, forgive me for the times my selfishness and disobedience have caused my mother to worry, feel sad, or felt disappointed in me. Help me to mature. Teach me the great benefits of obedience, and please grant me godly wisdom from above so that I am ever aware of my words and behavior. I desire to live according to your will and bring joy to you, my mother, and experience the good life you want me to enjoy. Thank you. Amen.

Let Us Learn the Spiritual Lesson: Isaiah 53:10 (The Living Bible) "But it was the LORD's good plan to crush [Jesus] and cause him grief. Yet when his life is made an offering for sin, he will have many descendants. He will enjoy a long life, and the LORD's good plan will prosper in his hands."

Let Us Reflect: What have you learned? What can you do better or differently now?

_____
_____
_____
_____
_____
_____
_____

Day 29

"Be Humble and Confident, Not Arrogant"

How easy it is to get beside yourself when you have succeeded in something. After a win, the natural response of too many people is to gloat over their success and bash the person who lost. Poor sportsmanship is not only unattractive; it shows gross immaturity. As my mama would say, "Be humble and confident, not arrogant." You won't win every time. How you treat others is the way you can expect to be treated when your time comes around.

Let Us Pray: Heavenly Father, thank you for sending your son, Jesus Christ, to teach me how to live in great confidence and complete humility. As I do my best to please you with every gift, talent, ability, and every blessing you give me, help me to always express gratitude to you and give you the glory. I will always give you the praise and celebrate others too.

Let Us Learn the Spiritual Lesson: James 4:5–6 (KJV)
"Do ye think that the scripture saith in vain, The spirit that dwelleth in us lusteth to envy? But he giveth more grace. Wherefore he saith, God resisteth the proud, but giveth grace unto the humble."

Let Us Reflect: What have you learned? What can you do better and differently now?

_____
_____
_____
_____
_____
_____
_____

Day 30

"Always Say What You Mean and Always Mean What You Say"

People cannot read your mind. My mama used to say, "Always say what you mean and always mean what you say." Whether people like it or not, you will be respected for being open and honest. If nothing more, respect yourself enough to be true to yourself. What you think, what you want, and how you feel are all within your power to control. Never give your power to another by being dishonest about your thoughts and feelings.

Let Us Pray: Father, I know you honor words. You speak truth and your words never fail. As you keep your word with me, teach me to only speak what I mean and keep my word with you and others too. Thank you for showing me your faithfulness. I commit to do the same in Jesus's name. Amen.

Let Us Learn the Spiritual Lesson: James 5:12 (NIV)
"Above all, my brothers and sisters, do not swear—not by heaven or by earth or by anything else. All you need to say is a simple 'Yes' or 'No.' Otherwise you will be condemned."

Let Us Reflect: What have you learned? What can you do better or differently now?

Day 31

"Don't Devalue Yourself by Lowering Your Standards or Compromising Your Principles for Nobody"

American poet E. E. Cummings said, "To be nobody but yourself in a world which is doing its best day and night to make you like everybody else means to fight the hardest battle which any human being can fight and never stop fighting." How true are his words? Very. I was often guilty of trying too hard to make people like me. I was the kid who wanted so very desperately to get along with everybody, which caused me to judge myself too harshly.

However, even in my desire to get along and have friends, I was never pushed to the point of lowering my standards and compromising myself or my standards. I was able to draw the line in the sand and not try to change so people would like and accept me for me. I owe that to my mother because she constantly drilled in my head and spirit these words, "Don't devalue yourself by lowering your standards or compromising your principles for nobody. If they don't like you, that's their loss."

Let Us Pray: Lord, my body and life belong to you. Thank you for giving me your word to guide my decisions and rule my life. As I commit to live according to your word, teach me how to resist feelings of discouragement when people fail to accept, love, and respect me for who I am. Even when they do not respond favorably to me, teach me to continue to stand firm with no compromise. Always help me to choose what pleases you over and above what others may want and require of me. I trust your word and I know you will teach me your ways always. Lord, thank you.

Let Us Learn the Spiritual Lesson: Romans 12:1–2 (NIV) "Therefore, I urge you, brothers and sisters, in view of God's mercy, to offer your bodies as a living sacrifice, holy and pleasing to God—this is your true and proper worship. Do not conform to the pattern of this world, but be transformed by the renewing of your mind. Then you will be able to test and approve what God's will is—his good, pleasing and perfect will."

Let Us Reflect: What have you learned? What can you do better or differently now?

_____
_____
_____
_____
_____
_____
_____

Segment 5: Expressed

For the waywardness of the simple will kill them, and the complacency of fools will destroy them; but whoever listens to me will live in safety and be at ease, without fear of harm.

— Proverbs 1:32–33 (NIV)

There is absolutely no way I could ever recall all the many words Mama spoke to me. Equally, recalling the exact time and place, and the reason for which my Mama spoke those words are vague at best. However, I always knew and felt my mother's actions and words were out of genuine love and sincere concern for me. I did not like her disciplinary actions nor did I always appreciate her corrective words, but I knew she loved me. I knew she cared. I knew she had my best interest at heart.

Included in this section are a few words that resonate with me the most; words Mama used to say that were intended to guide me and guard me. I pray as you read these next sayings you too will feel my love and concern for you. If you have also heard your mother speak the same words, thank God. They are for you because you are loved, and we have your best interest in mind.

Day 32

"I Brought You into This World, I Will Take You Out"

No long explanation is needed here. My mama did not play with her rules. She did not tolerate disobedience, sassiness, or disrespect. Whenever I said or did anything that was out of line, before giving me her iron-hand whippings, she would give me her evil eye and say, "Girl, don't try me. I brought you into this world and I will take you out." I would quickly go somewhere and shut up and sit down because I believed Mama would do just what she said.

Let Us Pray: Dear God, forgive me when I disobey your word. You show me mercy and grace when I need it most. Whenever my ways are upsetting to my mother and she shares her disappointment with me, I pray you will help me to understand her heart and properly communicate my apology and follow up with changed behavior. In Jesus's name. Amen.

Let Us Learn the Spiritual Lesson: Hebrews 12:5–7 (NIV) "My son, do not make light of the LORD's discipline, and do not lose heart when he rebukes you, because the LORD disciplines the one he loves, and he chastens everyone he accepts as his son. Endure hardship as discipline; God is treating you as his children. For what children are not disciplined by their father?"

Let Us Reflect: What have you learned? What can you do better or differently now?

_____
_____
_____
_____
_____
_____
_____

Day 33

"Do not Borrow What You Cannot Repay"

I was so excited to be moving out of my mother's house and getting my very own apartment. For months, I saved money and even put many household items in the layaway. By the time moving day finally came around, I still had many more items and furnishing I wanted to acquire but could not afford at the time. So I decided to open a few accounts to make purchases that I could not afford just so that I could have everything I wanted but did not necessarily need on moving day. I won't ever forget my mama saying to me, "Do not borrow what you cannot repay." If only I had listened to her advice then, I could have avoided years of struggling to pay bills that outlived the items I bought on credit.

Let Us Pray: Lord, thank you for providing all my needs and giving me many of my desires. Help me to manage my money well. When I borrow money and obtain credit, help me to do it responsibly and repay it timely. Amen.

Let Us Learn the Spiritual Lesson: Psalm 37:21–22 (KJV) "The wicked borrow and do not repay, but the righteous give generously; those the Lord blesses will inherit the land, but those he curses will be destroyed."

Let Us Reflect: What have you learned? What can you do better or differently now?

Day 34

"Do Not Let People Do More for You Than You Are Willing to Do for Them and Yourself"

Everybody knows somebody who is a "user," a person who always looks for and wants others to do something for them. Many times, what the users are asking of others, they can do themselves. They ask for stuff they do not need, already have, or what they can get for themselves. Users just like the idea of always being on the receiving end. My Mama had, and I imagine still has, a great disdain for people who use others. My mama still says to this day, "Do not let people do more for you than you are willing to do for them and yourself." Mama would generally end her rant by saying, "Nobody likes a user . . . and when people do too much for you, they will talk about you." I have lived long enough to see and share those same sentiments as my mother. God created us to help one another, not use each other.

Let Us Pray: Heavenly Father, help me always to treat others the way I desire to be treated. When others have shown me kindness, I pray you will also help me to quickly repay their good deeds. Keep your hands upon me so that I willingly and freely do good to others, and never withhold offering kind acts to them just as you extend your goodness and kindness to me. In Jesus's name I pray. Amen.

Let Us Learn the Spiritual Lesson: Matthew 7:11–12 (NIV) "If you, then, though you are evil, know how to give good gifts to your children, how much more will your Father in heaven give good gifts to those who ask him! So in everything, do to others what you would have them do to you, for this sums up the Law and the Prophets."

Let Us Reflect: What have you learned? What can you do better or differently now?

_____
_____
_____
_____
_____
_____
_____

Day 35

"Blood Is Thicker than Water, Family Is First"

The "blood of the covenant is thicker than the water of the womb," is a quote that refers to the bond between soldiers. Soldiers have a stronger bond between themselves than with their families of origin. When Mama said, "Blood is thicker than water, family is first," she was telling my siblings and I that no one should come between us. She was instilling within us loyalty for one another. From the time I was old enough to grasp her words and until now, in my heart, my love and commitment to my family comes first. After all, God gave us the family he wants us to have, and he allows us to choose our friends.

Let Us Pray: Lord, thank you for my family. Teach me to love, honor, and properly prioritize and take care of my family in the same manner you care for me. I pray in Jesus's name. Amen.

Let Us Learn the Spiritual Lesson: 1 Timothy 5:8 (NIV)
"Anyone who does not provide for their relatives, and especially for their own household, has denied the faith and is worse than an unbeliever."

Let Us Reflect: What have you learned? What can you do better or differently now?

_____
_____
_____
_____
_____
_____
_____

Day 36

"Do as I Say, Not as I Do"

No one must tell you there are no perfect and faultless people in the world, you know that all too well. My mama always told me the right thing to do, even if she failed to do it herself. On those rare occasions I saw my mother do something that was wrong, she would say, "Do as I say, not as I do." I thought those were the most hypocritical words someone could say, until I matured enough to understand the love behind the language. Just because a person knows the right thing to do does not mean they will always choose to do it. More so, just because a person fails to do the right thing does not mean they are unqualified to tell you the right thing to do. A wise person does what is right even when and if others choose otherwise. My mother loved me enough to want me to know right from wrong, and she wanted me to be wise enough to choose to do the right thing.

Let Us Pray: Lord, you are the only perfect, faultless, and sinless person who has ever and will ever walk the earth. Teach me to always follow you. Give me the wisdom and strength to do that which is right and pleasing in your sight, and not judge others for the choice they make. Thank you for loving me enough to put people in my life who will think enough of me to tell and show me the right way to go and the right things to do. I pray this prayer according to your righteous will, in Jesus's name. Amen.

Let Us Learn the Spiritual Lesson: Matthew 23:1–3 (NIV) "Then Jesus said to the crowds and to his disciples: 'The teachers of the law and the Pharisees sit in Moses' seat. So you must be careful to do everything they tell you. But do not do what they do, for they do not practice what they preach.'"

Let Us Reflect: What have you learned? What can you do better or differently now?

_____
_____
_____
_____
_____
_____
_____

Day 37

"To Hell with What People Think and Say, They Did Not Wake You Up This Morning"

Unfortunately, there are far too many people in the world who are ready to tear down your self-image, rain on your parade, and throw salt in your game. If you are not careful and prayerful, those people will cause you to think too little of yourself and too much about them. I cried far too many tears before I finally embraced the words my mama used to say. Whenever I cried to her about what somebody said or did to harm me, Mama would angrily say, "Girl, to hell with what people think and say, they did not wake you up this morning." Mama wanted me to understand that no one had or have power over my life, destiny, and future, unless I give them access into my mind. Their words brought fear and doubt, but Mama would reinforce the power I possessed if I did not allow people to get in my head and change my thinking. The only words to hear are God's words, and the only person to fear is God himself.

Let Us Pray: Heavenly Father, your word says you love me and your thoughts of me are great in number. Even when I fall and fail, you never cease to love and think well of me. Teach me to hear only words that will correct, build, encourage, and edify. Teach me to resist and rebuke anyone who seeks to break my spirit, discourage, deceive, minimize, and hurt me with their words and actions. I look to you, the only one greater than me, and with listening ears I hear only your voice speaking through others. Thank you for always speaking to me and sending your word to help me succeed in and eventually overcome the world. I pray in Jesus's name. Amen.

Let Us Learn the Spiritual Lesson: Luke 12:4–5 (NIV)
"I tell you, my friends, do not be afraid of those who kill the body and after that can do no more. But I will show you whom you should fear: Fear him who, after your body has been killed, has authority to throw you into hell. Yes, I tell you, fear him."

Let Us Reflect: What have you learned? What can you do better or differently now?

_____
_____
_____
_____
_____
_____
_____

Day 38

"If Your Friends Jump Off a Cliff, Will You Jump Off the Cliff Too"?

My mother was a single parent of three children who she was raising in a low-income neighborhood that many people would call "the ghetto." But our home was anything but a ghetto. It was no slum by far. My mother always worked a full-time job outside our home, but the work and hours she put into our home outnumbered any hours for which her employer cut her a paycheck. She taught us. She disciplined us. She challenged us. She praised us and asked questions of us that would make the smartest kid feel stupid. In fact, Mama one time asked, "If your friends jump off a cliff will you jump off the cliff too?" Before we could answer, she would quickly add, "Don't be stupid. Think for yourself. Use your brain."

Let Us Pray: Lord, you have blessed me with a good strong mind. Help me to think intelligently about everything and never rush to follow others in doing anything. Thank you for promising to lead and guide me in all that I do. Help me to trust you to lead me and resist following fools. I pray in Jesus's name. Amen.

Let Us Learn the Spiritual Lesson: Isaiah 30:1 (KJV)
"Woe to the rebellious children, saith the LORD, that take counsel, but not of me; and that cover with a covering, but not of my spirit, that they may add sin to sin:"

Let Us Reflect: What have you learned? What can you do better or differently now?

_____
_____
_____
_____
_____
_____
_____

Day 39

"Ain't Nobody Better than You, and You Ain't Better than Nobody . . . You Always Try to Better Yourself"

As a teen, I remember idolizing over a few people who I thought the world revolved around. I would go on and on and on telling my mother how great I thought they were. My mother would listen and agree with a few compliments, but she never let me keep praising others without saying something to remind me of my potential and greatness. Mama would say things like, "Ain't nobody better than you, and you ain't better than nobody . . . you just always try to better yourself." Those words I am so very glad my mother put into my spirit. She was teaching me to keep my focus on what God was doing in me, and to make self-improvement my priority. Complimenting others was always encouraged, but idolizing people was certainly frowned upon.

Let Us Pray: Father, you created everyone in your image, and you gave each person unique gifts and abilities for self-expression, and to give you glory. Thank you. As I continue to grow and come into a greater awareness of who I am and all the gifts and abilities you have given me, always teach me to give you my best. Help me to also appreciate the gifts and abilities of others and use me to encourage them to always give their best to you as well. In Jesus's name I ask and pray. Amen.

Let Us Learn the Spiritual Lesson: Luke 6:42 (NIV)
"How can you say to your brother, 'Brother, let me take the speck out of your eye,' when you yourself fail to see the plank in your own eye? You hypocrite, first take the plank out of your eye, and then you will see clearly to remove the speck from your brother's eye."

Let Us Reflect: What have you learned? What can you do better or differently now?

_____
_____
_____
_____
_____
_____
_____

Segment 6: Engaged

*We who are strong ought to bear with the failings
of the weak and not to please ourselves.*

—Romans 15:1 (NIV)

Daughters often complain that their mother does not listen, and she does not understand. For sure, there were many times during my childhood that I thought the same. Thankfully, God blessed me with a mother who not only gave instructions and punished me for infractions; she was a most engaging mother too. She took time to listen to me. In fact, more often than I wanted, my mother was engaging. She was big about making sure she listened to me and that I listened, understood, and obeyed her instructions as well.

As you have read thus far, there were many things my mother said that I did not understand. I did not understand on the same level as my mother because a child's mind just does not operate that way. But having a relationship that involved both talking and listening of each person was key to my growth, and it will be key to your growth as well. Learn to not only listen, but learn to talk. Learn not only to talk, but to listen. In other words, engage. The mother-daughter dyad will yield many hours, days, and years of happiness when you intentionally engage in healthy dialogue. Respect each other and learn to develop the type of friendship that God desires of mothers and daughters. I am glad my mother and I did. We did and we still do! Engage!

Day 40

"Don't Let Anyone Tell You What You Cannot Do, You Can Do Whatever You Put Your Mind to Do"

It was so easy to quit when no one thought I could do what I failed at doing anyway. It was easy, but my mother never let me do it. Quitting was not an option. If I joined something and discovered I did not like it or was not good at it, my mother made me finish the course. Cake decorating, sewing, jazz dance, tap dance, basketball, volleyball, tennis, swimming, flute, clarinet, bass clarinet, and piano lessons, are just some of the activities I discovered I was not the best at, but I could not quit until the class or lessons or season was over.

From the time I expressed interest until I finally decided it was not for me, I would hear my mama say time and time again, "Don't let anyone tell you what you cannot do. You can do whatever you put your mind to do." Mama was right. I discovered I could do anything, even when I decided I no longer liked or wanted to do it.

Let Us Pray: Lord, thank you for giving me a mind and the mental fortitude to recreate and envision. Thank you for giving me the strength, power, and physical ability to do things. In whatever I think, imagine, or do, let it not all be for my personal gain and satisfaction, but in all things, I pray it is for your glory. In Jesus's name I pray. Amen.

Let Us Learn the Spiritual Lesson: Genesis 11:6 (NIV)
"The LORD said, "If as one people speaking the same language they have begun to do this, then nothing they plan to do will be impossible for them."

Let Us Reflect: What have you learned? What can you do better or differently now?

_____
_____
_____
_____
_____
_____
_____

Day 41

"The More I Teach You the Dumber I Get"

Yes, Mama got jokes. Whenever I totally messed up on some directive she gave, or misunderstood a point Mama made, she would rush to make a facetious remark. Mama said, "The more I teach you the dumber I get." Even while joking, Mama was teaching me a lesson. She was teaching me to not only hear, but also listen and pay attention.

Let Us Pray: Father, I thank you for loving me enough to instruct me. As I commit to read and obey your word, I pray you will give me wisdom and understanding to correctly apply your word to my life. Thank you in advance for the promises that are sure to follow my obedience. I pray this prayer in Jesus's name. Amen.

Let Us Learn the Spiritual Lesson: Jeremiah 7: 23–26 (NIV) "but I gave them this command: Obey me, and I will be your God and you will be my people. Walk in obedience to all I command you, that it may go well with you. But they did not listen or pay attention; instead, they followed the stubborn inclinations of their evil hearts. They went backward and not forward. From the time your ancestors left Egypt until now, day after day, again and again I sent you my servants the prophets. But they did not listen to me or pay attention."

Let Us Reflect: What have you learned? What can you do better or differently now?

Day 42

"If It Were A Snake It Would've Bitten You"

Interrupting my playtime to come get something that was usually just a few feet, if not inches, away from my mother was annoying. My mother wasted no time calling me to come get the remote control, pour her a glass of water, or something that I could not understand why she couldn't have done herself. In my haste to get back to play, or whatever I was doing before my mother called my name, I would sometimes yell back, "I don't see it." Sometimes my mother would say, "Keep looking." At other times she would say, "If I get up and find it, I'm going to whip your butt." Other times, my mother would get up and look wherever she told me to look. I remember my mother holding object after object in her hand and saying, "If it is a snake it would've bit you."

Shamefully, I can now freely admit, most times I did not care to find the object anyway, but my mother was saying to me to be more observant. Do not miss what is obvious. Do not overlook what is within your view. God is always near. God's blessings are all around us, but sometimes we miss his blessings because we are distracted by our own selfishness.

Let Us Pray: Lord, you are so good to me. Whatever you ask me to do is all for my good and your glory. Teach me to observe your ways and obey your words. I repent for all the times I have complained and failed to thank you for all the blessings you have showered on me. Teach me to walk in the Spirit and not according to my sight, so I won't miss what you are doing in, around, and through me. I pray and sincerely ask you to help me in Jesus's name. Amen.

Let Us Learn the Spiritual Lesson: Isaiah 40:26 (NIV)
"Lift up your eyes and look to the heavens: Who created all these? He who brings out the starry host one by one and calls forth each of them by name. Because of his great power and mighty strength, not one of them is missing."

Let Us Reflect: What have you learned? What can you do better or differently now?

_____
_____
_____
_____
_____
_____
_____

Day 43

"Put Some Money Away for a Rainy Day"

Whether it's money in a savings account, countless brown pennies lined up on her dresser, or a plethora of silver dimes in jars, even when my mother claims to be broke, she always has some money somewhere. My mother told me time after time, "Mimi, put some money away for a rainy day." She told me if I learned how to save money that one day my money would save me. Boy, was she right. My mother was right for trying to teach me good money management skills, but again, I did not always listen or understand what Mama used to say.

I rush to say, a hard head and countless bad decisions helped me learn some lessons the hard way. As sure as there are sunny days, rainy days will come and the person who spends every dime they have today will find themselves left out in the rain tomorrow.

Earn money.
Get money.
Save money.
Period.

Let Us Pray: Lord, your word says you will give me power to get wealth that you may establish your covenant with me. Help me properly manage every blessing you send my way and to save more than I spend. I desire to honor you in all things, especially my tangible blessings.

Forgive me for the times I have not done so and please grant me mercy and more opportunities to honor you with my money now, in Jesus's name I pray. Amen.

Let Us Learn the Spiritual Lesson: Ecclesiastes 10:19 (NIV) "A feast is made for laughter, wine makes life merry, and money is the answer for everything."

Proverbs 6:6–8 (NIV)
"Go to the ant, you sluggard; consider its ways and be wise! It has no commander, no overseer or ruler, yet it stores its provisions in summer and gathers its food at harvest."

Let Us Reflect: What have you learned? What can you do better or differently now?

_____
_____
_____
_____
_____
_____
_____

Day 44

"Always Wear Clean Underwear because You Never Know When You Might End Up in an Accident"

Honestly, my sister, I still have no clue exactly what my mother meant when she regularly asked, "Are you wearing clean underwear?" and followed up with "Always wear clean underwear because you never know when you might end up in an accident." What I do know is during my high school and college years, she spoke those words to me quite often. If you know what those words mean please send me an email or something, will you?

Let Us Pray: Lord, I know my body is the place where your Holy Spirit lives. Thank you for trusting me with the honor of representing you on earth. I pray you will teach and continually impress upon my heart to daily love, care for, and respect my body as your dwelling place. May my self-expression through the under and outer garments I choose to wear always properly and respectfully represent you, my Heavenly Father. I pray in Jesus's name. Amen.

Let Us Learn the Spiritual Lesson: Exodus 19:10–11 (KJV) "And the LORD said to Moses, 'Go to the people and consecrate them today and tomorrow. Have them wash their clothes and be ready by the third day, because on that day the LORD will come down on Mount Sinai in the sight of all the people.'"

Let Us Reflect: What have you learned? What can you do better or differently now?

_____
_____
_____
_____
_____
_____
_____

Day 45

"You Will Miss Me When I'm Gone"

Thankfully, whenever my mother said, "You will miss me when I'm gone," she was purposely trying to make me feel guilty for doing or saying something silly. I thank God for the uniquely special friendship my mother and I share. Almost daily, we laugh and share so many wonderful conversations. We argue back and forth about who is the funniest and the wittiest.

It rarely fails. Whenever I tell a joke (at her expense) or pointed out one of her quirky actions, Mama will quickly say, "That's okay, you will miss me when I'm gone." Her defensive comment causes me to laugh harder, but her words also cause me to feel a little somber later. Yep, that is one of her dirty tricks to win, but her words ring loud and clear. They are true. Mothers and daughters do not have forever to enjoy one another. It would be wise to live each day as if it were our last because one day it will be.

Let Us Pray: Lord, every day of my life, please help me to see and appreciate every blessing you have given me, most especially the blessing of having my mother. Help me watch my mouth so that I never disrespect her with my words and help me to prioritize my days so that I never overlook her needs and miss sharing quality time with her. I honestly pray this prayer in Jesus's name. Amen.

Let Us Learn the Spiritual Lesson: John 7:33–34 (NIV)
"Jesus said, 'I am with you for only a short time, and then I am going to the one who sent me. You will look for me, but you will not find me; and where I am, you cannot come.'"

Let Us Reflect: What have you learned? What can you do better or differently now?

_____
_____
_____
_____
_____
_____
_____

Day 46

"Learn to Listen and You Won't Have to Regret Saying My Mama Told Me So"

My first year in college was so exciting. I was excited about meeting new people, experiencing new things, and being a grown-up! My mother bought my first car in the last semester of high school, but she did not allow me to drive it to school. In fact, she did not allow me to drive it any farther than the neighborhood corner store. But in my first year in college, she finally gave me permission to drive to college and back, forty minutes away! I had a license, I had a car, and I had permission to drive. I was finally a grown-up! I will never forget my mama asking at least once a week, "Mimi, do you have enough gas in that car? Don't be taking chances. Stop and get gas before it gets dark . . ." I heard the same questions weekly, but Mama's words fell on deaf ears.

I was grown. I knew how to handle my business, at least I thought. On the way to school one morning, I ran out of gas and was on the side of the road with not one penny in my pocket. I was broke. I had no gas. I had to call my mama. Boy, was I embarrassed. When Mama came, I was surprised that I didn't get fussed at or the keys taken. She looked at me and ever so sincerely and compassionately said, "Learn to listen and you won't have to regret saying Mama told me so." I simply replied, "You did tell me." My mother was trying to save me from unnecessary pain, problems, inconvenience, and possible danger.

Let Us Pray: Lord, thank you for sending your word to guide me around pitfalls. I repent for all the times I have disobeyed and ignored godly advice and good motherly instruction. Thank you for healing and helping me get over the hurt and problems I caused myself. Help me to mature and teach me obedience. I ask this in Jesus's name. Amen.

Let Us Learn the Spiritual Lesson: Luke 24:6–8 (NIV)
"He is not here; he has risen! Remember how he told you, while he was still with you in Galilee: 'The Son of Man must be delivered over to the hands of sinners, be crucified and on the third day be raised again.' Then they remembered his words."

Let Us Reflect: What have you learned? What can you do better or differently now?

_____
_____
_____
_____
_____
_____
_____

Day 47

"Get the Lead Out of Your Butt"

From my earliest recollection until now, I have never seen my mother not work. She has never been a lazy person. Even in her seventies, she rarely sits around and do nothing unless she is sick, and even while sick she is pushing herself to do more than she should. There is not one lazy bone in her body. Oh, how I wish she had at least one lazy bone or two because whenever she was working, she made us work too.

Very early every Saturday morning, on holidays, and school breaks, my mother would pull back the curtains, open the mini blinds, turn on the lights, and yell, "Get up, it's time to clean up . . . get up right now. Do you think you are going to sleep all day?" Lord, have mercy. So many days I wanted to scream or hide under the bed or in the closet. I wanted to just sleep longer, but my mama was not having it. Washing and ironing, cooking and cleaning, washing and combing and pressing hair, and etc., in my mama's mind there was always something to do. If I moved too slow or took too long getting up my mama would yell, "Get the lead out of your butt."

My mother was teaching me the value of hard work. When Mama said get the lead out of your butt, she was telling me to hurry up, to stop wasting time, to quit letting anything get in my way of progress and doing what I needed to do. What my mother was teaching me was how to seize the day and not allow slothfulness to rob me of the opportunities good time management and hard work are sure to present.

Let Us Pray: Heavenly Father, even through your holy word you teach me how to manage my day and time well. In six days, you created the whole world and everything in it according to your perfect plan and order. Please help me do the same. Teach me to order, plan, and work each day so that I too can enjoy the fruit of my labor and enjoy the works of my hands. I commit my plans and my work to you. Thank you in advance for helping me do all things well. In Jesus's name I pray. Amen.

Let Us Learn the Spiritual Lesson: Proverbs 6:9–11 (KJV) "How long wilt thou sleep, O sluggard? when wilt thou arise out of thy sleep? Yet a little sleep, a little slumber, a little folding of the hands to sleep: So shall thy poverty come as one that travelleth, and thy want as an armed man."

Let Us Reflect: What have you learned? What can you do better or differently now?

_____
_____
_____
_____
_____
_____
_____

Segment 7: Excited

Yet I will rejoice in the Lord, *I will joy in the God of my salvation.*
—Habakkuk 3:18 (KJV)

Merriam Webster defines "excited" as "very enthusiastic and eager." When my spirit was low, my mother was a cheerleader. When my faith was failing, my mother was a preacher. When my vision was dim, my mother was a visionary coach. My mother was not perfect, I am certain I have intimated that already, but she was and remains to be the perfect mother to and for me. More than any other emotion, my mother stirs up a feeling of excitement for me. She knows just what to say and when to say what I need to hear.

My God, the older I get and the more I reflect upon my childhood experiences, the more thankful I become. My mother molded me to love, to believe, to dream, to work, to love, to believe, to dream, to work, to love, to believe, to dream, to work. No, you are not reading a typo. The repetition is intentional, although each time I wrote the words I was excited and had a different thought. I kept thinking about the words my mother said and say to this day that have kept me moving forward during the darkest and most uncertain times of my life, and I want to repeat the words all over again. Mothers are God's gift to daughters; and just as Jesus is the joy of salvation, mothers who teach and encourage their daughters evoke a sense of joy and energy for life! Mothers and daughters share the excitement for life, in life, about life! Words are powerful to excite!

Day 48

"Dream Big, the Sky Is the Limit"

I had just written a gospel stage play and did not really know what to do with it. I had written many short skits for churches and even the Baptist convention, but that was about as far as it went. This time, I wanted to do it all, but I did not know exactly what that meant. I was in my late twenties, and I remember telling my mother I wanted to put my play at a community center. She looked at me and said, "Dream big, the sky is the limit. You can do whatever you want to do, baby." I am sure she had spoken those words countless times before, but that day, I heard her. I heard her, and I believed her.

I purchased numerous tickets and spent countless dollars patronizing other playwrights over the years. I was in the audience to witness the great work and talent of far too many actors, actresses, and artists to count. The venues amazed me. The lights and cameras excited me, but nothing could compare to my mama's words that finally inspired me to "dream big, the sky is the limit."

A few years later, not only had I written, directed, and produced my own work, but I was blessed to debut my play at one of the most exclusive venues in Houston. Without a team, no accountants, marketing professionals, or renowned actors or experienced businessmen, God helped me to do exactly what I desired to do. My name was on the marquee. The title of my play was in lights in one of the greatest theater districts in the nation, and the fourth largest city in the country. Finally, my work and dreams were scratching the surface of many more great platforms I have yet to mount. Dream and dream big.

Let Us Pray: Lord, you are a great God and you do all things well. I pray for your spirit to live fully and freely in me. Help me see as you see and think your thoughts. Because nothing is too hard for you, help me to walk in total confidence knowing that nothing shall be impossible for me. Today, I put all my trust in you and commit to giving my best, thinking and expecting the best because you give me your best. In Jesus's name. Amen.

Let Us Learn the Spiritual Lesson: Ephesians 3:20 (KJV)
"Now unto Him that is able to do exceeding abundantly above all that we ask or think, according to the power that worketh in us."

Let Us Reflect: What have you learned? What can you do better or differently now?

_____
_____
_____
_____
_____
_____
_____

Day 49

"If You Want It Get It, You Can Have Whatever You Want"

It was the summer of 2002. Against all the odds that were stacked against me, God blessed me to have a home built from the ground up. Well, at the time it was only a promise because no mortgage deed had been signed. The builders were in the final days of finishing construction. The realtor scheduled a day for me to come into the studio to pick out the furnishing. My mother agreed to join me. As we walked through the studio, looking at cabinets, carpet swatches, brick and roof samples, I was more than a little overwhelmed. I was overwhelmed because I did not have the best credit score. I did not have any money in my savings account, and I only had a part-time job at the church where I was employed. I was overwhelmed but was walking by faith. God told me he was going to bless me with my own home, and I believed him. I believed God, but every now and then doubt crept into my mind.

The young lady had a clipboard and pen in her hand. She was rattling off question after question as we walked through the studio. Obviously, my hesitation in answering alerted my mother to speak up. My mother pulled my arm and looked me straight in the eyes as if she wanted to calm my spirit. I knew God was speaking to my doubt when I heard Mama say, "If you want it get it, you can have whatever you want." I heard God. I believed God. I heard what Mama said. My mother was saying that God will bless me with my desires if I trust and obey him. Seventeen years later and I am living in the house that God promised to give me. I am still enjoying everything I desired to have because God is good, and God is faithful.

Let Us Pray: Lord, not because I deserve anything but because you are my Heavenly Father, I know you will always take care of me and give me the things I desire that are in line with your will and plan. Thank you for loving me like you do. Help me to rest in your love and always walk in full assurance that you will bless me according to your goodness and riches in glory. In Jesus's name, I pray. Amen.

Let Us Learn the Spiritual Lesson: Matthew 7:11 (KJV)
"If ye then, being evil, know how to give good gifts unto your children, how much more shall your Father which is in heaven give good things to them that ask him!"

Let Us Reflect: What have you learned? What can you do better or differently now?

_____
_____
_____
_____
_____
_____
_____

Day 50

"Better Days Are Coming"

Heartbroken. Heartbroken by someone I loved and trusted. The tears rolled uncontrollably down my cheeks and my heart was filled with anguish, disappointment, and pain—pain like I had never known as a child, teen, or even as a young adult. I was in my forties and still needed to hear the comforting words of my mama saying to me, "Better days are coming." I was preaching and teaching the word of God. I was encouraging, counseling, and helping men, women, and children understand and get past their difficult moments and painful predicaments. But when I experienced a pain I had never known, I could not seem to pull myself together.

Many days I felt like a helpless and powerless girl who needed her mother, and every time I called on my mother, she was there. When I *did not* call, she was there. Sometimes I did not want her there to see me in such a weak place, but my mother was there for me unconditionally. Some days she said nothing at all. Other days, she said more than I wanted to hear, but thank God whenever Mama said, "Better days are coming" somehow, I knew and trusted she was right. Mama, after all, had already been in the position I was in on more than one occasion.

Thank God I believed my mama and trusted my God. No matter how hard and difficult it may be, just as God promised and like what Mama said, indeed, better days are coming. Never give up. Never quit. Choose to live to see another day.

Let Us Pray: Heavenly Father, as long as you are with me I know that all things will work for my good. When I am sad, cheer me up. When I am low, lift me up. When I am discouraged, encourage me. When I am hurt, heal me. I am yours, Lord, and I trust you to take care of me always. Thank you, Lord. In Jesus's name I pray. Amen.

Let Us Learn the Spiritual Lesson: Psalm 30:4–5 (NIV)
"Sing the praises of the **LORD**, you his faithful people; praise his holy name. For his anger lasts only a moment, but his favor lasts a lifetime; weeping may stay for the night, but rejoicing comes in the morning."

Let Us Reflect: What have you learned? What can you do better or differently now?

_____
_____
_____
_____
_____
_____
_____

Day 51

"Love Yourself and Follow Your Heart"

I confess, Monday, January 21, 2019 at 3:53 p.m., without telling her why I was asking, I called my mother to ask what one thing she would say to me again. After she asked me several questions, she finally said to me the same words she had spoken so many times when I was a young girl. Mama said, "Love yourself and follow your heart . . ." Mama started preaching about why self-love is so important. She raised her voice and was going in, until I finally said, "Okay, okay. Thank you, Mama." She tickles me. She answered the question as if she had never spoken those words to me before. I was not in my feelings when I called, but after talking to her, I felt empowered. Inspired. Loved.

It is just something so liberating and uplifting about hearing your mother speak affirming words. Hearing a mother speak to her daughter should sound like the voice of the angel of God who spoke to Mary the mother of Jesus. Every daughter should feel like she is "blessed among women." Blessed girls and women know they are loved and that translates to self-love. A healthy self-love is liberating. Self-love will cause you to not only know you are loved and believe you deserve the best. Self-love will cause you to follow your heart and pursue all the great things life affords you.

Let Us Pray: Lord, thank you for loving me. Help me to love myself. As your love influences my heart, give me the faith and boldness to follow that which will bring joy and gladness. May you always guide me and find joy in all that I pursue. I pray in the name of Jesus. Amen.

Let Us Learn the Spiritual Lesson: Ecclesiastes 11:9 (KJV) "Rejoice, O young man, in thy youth; and let thy heart cheer thee in the days of thy youth, and walk in the ways of thine heart, and in the sight of thine eyes: but know thou, that for all these things God will bring thee into judgment."

Let Us Reflect: What have you learned? What can you do better or differently now?

_____
_____
_____
_____
_____
_____

Day 52

"Be a Leader"

My mother had a very low tolerance for certain behaviors. Too many times to mention, I tried to blame my misbehavior on my sister or brother. I would often say, "They made me do it" or "I did it (whatever it was) because everybody else was doing it." My mother would almost hit the roof in rage. Even if a butt whipping did not happen, she was most definitely going to say, "You be a leader." She would go on ranting about not allowing anyone to force me to do anything. She told me, "If you get your butt whooped for doing wrong, let it be because you wanted to do it and not because somebody made you do it. Be a leader." When I tell you I learned the lesson, I heard those words, believe me.

It is within every person's power to say yes and no. You can and should take charge of your thoughts, words, and deeds. You should live your life in such a way that others want to follow you. In life, you won't always be the leader, but how you choose to live will cause others to be drawn to you or be driven from you. Without a title or position, you are a leader. Choose to live by upright morals, principles, and obey good rules, so by your example others will be led well.

Let Us Pray: Because of your great leadership, Lord, I say thank you. I pray that even as Jesus demonstrated great leadership, you will teach me to listen, learn, and lead others to you as I follow you myself. Thank you for inviting me to accept Jesus as my Savior. As he leads me, I pray my life will cause others to be drawn to you in Jesus's name I pray. Amen.

Let Us Learn the Spiritual Lesson: Titus 2:7–8 (NIV)
"In everything set them an example by doing what is good. In your teaching show integrity, seriousness and soundness of speech that cannot be condemned, so that those who oppose you may be ashamed because they have nothing bad to say about us."

Let Us Reflect: What have you learned? What can you do better or differently now?

_____
_____
_____
_____
_____
_____
_____

Segment 8: Evolve

But now, by dying to what once bound us, we have been released from the law so that we serve in the new way of the Spirit, and not in the old way of the written code.

—Romans 7:6 (NIV)

To develop gradually over a period, especially from a simple to a more complex form, is the definition of evolve. Change. Everybody and everything will experience change, consciously and unconsciously, intentionally and unintentionally. Change is inevitable. Change is good. Change can be bad, but whether good or bad, change is a natural part of the cycle of life. Because change is so necessary yet resisted, I have listed several quotes from some of the world's most noted females, followed by words my mama used to say. Take time to read and meditate over the words and apply them to your life where needed, so that you can truly evolve into the person God intends and you desire.

> If you don't like something, change it. If you can't change it, change your attitude.
>
> —Maya Angelou

> Every time you state what you want or believe, you're the first to hear it. It's a message to both you a n d others about what you think is possible. Don't put a ceiling on yourself.
>
> —Oprah Winfrey

You can't make decisions based on fear and the possibility of what might happen.
—Former US First Lady Michelle Obama

Every great dream begins with a dreamer. Always remember, you have within you the strength, the patience, and the passion to reach for the stars to change the world.
—Harriet Tubman

I have learned over the years that when one's mind is made up, this diminishes fear; knowing what must be done does away with fear."
—Rosa Parks

Instead of looking at the past, I put myself ahead twenty years and try to look at what I need to do now in order to get there then."
—Diana Ross

Mature as a mother. Mature as a daughter. Mature enough to be honest with yourself about the changes that need to be made in you, with you, and around you so that you can become the best *you* that you can become. Today is a good day to evolve on purpose. My mama helped me begin the lifelong process of change, and I am gladly evolving. I invite you to evolve with me.

Day 53

"You Are a Blessing"

I think it is in every child's DNA to want to please their parents and to make their parents smile. I was no different. I wanted to please my mother, to see her smile, and to hear her say, "I am proud of you." Even today, as my ultimate aim is to please my Heavenly Father, but I still want to see my mother smile and to hear her say I am proud of you, but those words pale in comparison to hearing my mama say, "You are a blessing." That language speaks volumes for me. As a follower of Christ, I have come to understand that in pleasing God sometimes means others will find reasons to be displeased and unhappy with me. People do not always embrace those who strive to please that God, that great audience of one. Yet still I strive. I try. I fail. I admit my faults and weaknesses to God and keep on striving.

I was about twenty-nine years of age when I first recall hearing my mama say, "You are a blessing." We were walking out of a local department store and bumped into a church member. The older lady from church began praising my mother for raising a good daughter, her exact words. As she was sharing kind words about me, before she finished her statements, my mother took over the conversation. I heard my mother interjecting praiseworthy comments about me. When their conversation finally ended, my mother and I got into the car. I call myself getting my mother straight. I told my mother it was rude and rather embarrassing to hear her go on and on bragging about what a good daughter I am. My mother kindly let me finish talking, but immediately replied, "You are a blessing, and nobody knows that better than me. You cannot tell me what not to say. You are my child, and I am proud to let everybody know you are a blessing." Tears. Tears. Tears of joy were swelling in my eyes, but I did not let them roll down my face. I still needed my mother to understand how I felt. Each time I pressed my argument, she pressed hers and finally convinced me to concede. She was not going to let me win that argument. She ended the conversation by saying, "I also know you are not perfect." Whelp, there you have it. Being a blessing is not about being perfect, but it is about doing your best to live in a way that others appreciate you and your contributions to the family, work, school, and wherever you interact with people. No, God has not called us to please people, but when we obey his word, people will see us and say, "You are a blessing." God has certainly blessed you to be a blessing. So? Bless others!

Let Us Pray: Heavenly Father, for every blessing you have given me, thank you. Because life is a blessing, help me to live my life to reflect your goodness to others. In my words and by my actions, teach me to please you and help me to rest in knowing others will be blessed by my life and example. I pray in faith and with thanksgiving in Jesus name. Thank you for making me a blessing. Amen.

Let Us Learn the Spiritual Lesson: Genesis 12:1–3 (NKJV) "Now the LORD had said to Abram: 'Get out of your country, from your family and from your father's house, to a land that I will show you. I will make you a great nation; I will bless you and make your name great; And you shall be a blessing. I will bless those who bless you, And I will curse him who curses you; And in you all the families of the earth shall be blessed.'"

Let Us Reflect: What have you learned? What can you do better or differently now?

Day 54

"Don't Leave Out This House and Do Anything That Will Bring Shame to My Name Because You Are a Reflection of Me"

I do not know why this devotion topic caused me to laugh aloud, but it did. I heard the voice of one of my friends of over thirty years, "Lord, Lord, Lord, Lord, Lord, Lord, Lord, Lord." When we are discussing situations or news that is beyond our explanation, she will usually repeat those words, and we laugh, and the mood and tone of our conversation changes, and we laugh. How can I laugh when I think about my mama saying, "Don't leave out this house and do anything that will bring shame to my name because you are a reflection of me"? I really do not know because my mother was never joking when she threatened me with those words. On more than one occasion, my mother put a leather belt on my bottom because I acted up in public.

My mother was teaching me honor and respect. Because she laid down her rules and made sure I understood them; to go outside the home and do anything that was contrary to what she taught was an embarrassment and direct insult to her. She was teaching me that people would have certain expectations of me because of my relationship to her; that when people see me, they should be able to see similarities of her. When you fail, rather than cry, complain, blame, or hide behind your actions, it would be a great practice to call on the name of Jesus. By simply saying,

"Lord, Lord, Lord, Lord, Lord, Lord, Lord, Lord," you too might feel and sense a change in the atmosphere. Call him, do not shame him!

Let Us Pray: Lord, so many times I dishonor you by the way I talk and act. I confess my ways do not always reflect you or your goodness to me, forgive me. Forgive me and help me to pattern my life after Jesus, your son, who always properly represented you. I pray in Jesus's name. Amen.

Let Us Learn the Spiritual Lesson: Ezekiel 36:21–23 (NIV) "I had concern for my holy name, which the people of Israel profaned among the nations where they had gone. Therefore, say to the Israelites, 'This is what the Sovereign LORD says: It is not for your sake, people of Israel, that I am going to do these things, but for the sake of my holy name, which you have profaned among the nations where you have gone. I will show the holiness of my great name, which has been profaned among the nations, the name you have profaned among them. Then the nations will know that I am the LORD, declares the Sovereign LORD, when I am proved holy through you before their eyes.'"

Let Us Reflect: What have you learned? What can you do better or differently now?

_____
_____
_____
_____
_____
_____
_____

Day 55

"You Are a Good Woman"

For no apparent reason, my mama said, "You are a good woman." We were just out and about shopping and running errands, and my mother felt the need to compliment me. I said, "Thank you, but what did I do?" She immediately replied, "What don't you do, Mimi? You are always doing something for somebody. You are a good woman and daughter, and aunt. You are just good now." I was tickled. Even when giving compliments, my mother sometimes comes across as if she is fussing. I love it! No, I recant. I don't love when she comes off as if she is fussing, but I do love her *oho* so much! Trust me, your mother is your biggest cheerleader and hardest coach. Listen to her.

Let Us Pray: Lord, teach both mother and daughter how to practice doing good so that others may see and give glory to you. When and where we fail, thank you for giving us another chance. In Jesus's name. Amen.

Let Us Learn the Spiritual Lesson: Proverbs 31:10 (KJV)
"Who can find a virtuous woman? for her price is far above rubies."

Let Us Reflect: What have you learned? What can you do better or differently now?

_____
_____
_____
_____
_____
_____
_____

Day 56

"You Are a Beautiful Person"

"Girl, I have never seen a person who loves the mirror more than you do. It is pitiful. You are a beautiful person, but Lord have mercy," she said. We were on a cruise and everywhere we went, she was a few steps ahead. I was always the last to leave the cabin. After all, who can pass up taking one last look in the mirror? My mama was tired of waiting on me, but even in fussing, she found a way to compliment me.

Of course, it is important to look your best outwardly, but nothing is more important than working to beautify the inner you. However, having a mother to compliment you is important for a girl's self-esteem. Compliment others often. Whether mother, daughter, sister, or friend, every woman needs that positive energy. Thank God for those who give it. Be wise enough to receive and believe it too! You are beautiful. God created everybody, and when he looked at his work, God said "It is very good." I believe God. Don't you?

Let Us Pray: Lord, even before the world was created, you knew who and how you would create everybody and everything in it. Since you have created me, help me to see the same beauty you see. Thank you for creating and loving the me. Amen.

Let Us Learn the Spiritual Lesson: Song of Solomon 1:4–6 (NIV) "We rejoice and delight in you; we will praise your love more than wine. How right they are to adore you! Dark am I, yet lovely, daughters of Jerusalem, dark like the tents of Kedar, like the tent curtains of Solomon. Do not stare at me because I am dark, because I am darkened by the sun."

Let Us Reflect: What have you learned? What can you do better or differently now?

_____
_____
_____
_____
_____
_____
_____

Day 57

"I Am So Proud of You"

Every time I brought home an A on my report card, or brought up that C on my progress report, I heard my mama say, "I am so proud of you." When I tried out for the flagettes, the basketball, and volleyball team and made it, my mama said, "I am so proud of you." When I entered the modeling pageant and lost, my mama said, "I am so proud of you, you tried." When I totally botched the dress in my sewing class, my mama said, "That's okay. That's okay. I am so proud of you. You can't sew but you tried." When I brought home my first paycheck from Burger King, bought my first car, purchased my house, accepted my call to the preaching ministry, lost a pound or two, etcetera, etcetera, my mother would rush to say, "I am so proud of you."

If I had a dollar each time I heard my mother say those words, I would now be a billionaire. The fact that I heard and still hear my mother saying those words makes me rich. My mother intentionally encourages, affirms, and reaffirms me. She did it as a child, and she is still doing it today. Truly, a mother's love and support a wise daughter won't ever despise, reject, or outgrow.

Speak those words to your daughter. Embrace those words as a daughter. Speak those words to others, they are most powerful.

Let Us Pray: Father, thank you for the gift of mother. Teach me to love her the way she needs and deserves to be loved, honored, and respected. Help me always to be patient and understanding with her like you understand and extend your patience to me is my prayer in Jesus's name. Amen.

Let Us Learn the Spiritual Lesson: Proverbs 23:22 (NIV) "Listen to your father, who gave you life, and do not despise your mother when she is old."

Proverbs 3:12 (KJV) "For whom the LORD loveth he correcteth; even as a father the son in whom he delighteth."

Let Us Reflect: What have you learned? What can you do better or differently now?

_____
_____
_____
_____
_____
_____
_____

Day 58

"You Make Me So Happy"

Lord, who would have thought that the person who whipped my butt and lectured me seemingly without end could also be my closest friend? I am so thankful for the relationship my mother and I share. We play together. Laugh at and with each other. We vacation together. We cry sad tears together and help to share one another's burdens. Yes, my friendship with my mother is one of my greatest blessings. To hear Mama say, "You make me so happy" makes me the happiest woman on earth. I know real joy can only come from God, but we do have the power and influence to bring happiness to others. My mother certainly does that for me, and I thank God from her own lips I have often heard my mama say to me, "You make me so happy."

One of the main reasons for writing this devotional is because I truly believe God wants mothers and daughters to share a mutually healthy and fulfilling relationship, the kind of relationship my mother and I happily share.

Let Us Pray: Lord, help me to love her the way you love me so that our relationship models the same kind of relationship you have with your son and my Savior. In Jesus's name I pray. Amen.

Let Us Learn the Spiritual Lesson: Proverbs 23:25 (NIV)
"May your father and mother rejoice; may she who gave you birth be joyful!"

Let Us Reflect: What have you learned? What can you do better or differently now?

Day 59

"I Love You"

Almost every day of my adult life, I hear my mama say, "I love you." I am sure she probably said those words often during my childhood too. But my fifty-year-old memory won't allow me to make that claim now. What I do know and can honestly say is a few words are more meaningful to me. To hear Mama say "I love you" verbally, and to see her show those words in her selfless acts are like wind beneath my wings. I am writing these words while at home under the weather. Even though I begged my mother to stay home, while lying in bed, I saw a cane land on my top stair. I heard my mother (who suffers from back pain every day of her life) grunting and a few seconds after seeing the cane, I saw my mother finally make her way to the top of the stairs to my bed. I was totally frustrated because I begged her not to come. But after climbing sixteen stairs, with bated breath, I heard my mama say, "I love you, I had to come and see about you." There is no earthly love like a mother's love. I am persuaded.

Let Us Pray: Lord, thank you for blessing me with a mother who loves me. Help me to honor, respect, and daily show, and prove my love for her, too. In Jesus's name I pray. Amen.

Let Us Learn the Spiritual Lesson: 2 Samuel 21:9–10 (KJV) "And he delivered them into the hands of the Gibeonites, and they hanged them in the hill before the LORD: so they all fell seven together, and were put to death in the days of harvest, in the first days, in the beginning of barley harvest. And Rizpah the daughter of Aiah took sackcloth, and spread it for her upon the rock, from the beginning of harvest until water dropped upon them out of heaven; and suffered neither the birds of the air to rest on them by day nor the beasts of the field by night."

Let Us Reflect: What have you learned? What can you do better or differently now?

Day 60

"You Can Rest When I Die Knowing You Have Taken Good Care of Me"

I always try to avoid conversations about dying, although I know it is inevitable. Only God knows who will die first, but for sure I know that when that day comes, death will cause pain and a void that no one else will ever be able to fill; only God will be able to heal. My mother, in all her wisdom, never ceases to make my siblings and I engage in the hard conversations. Sometimes when we are riding around time just talking, my mother will strike up the dreaded conversation, and I do my best to change the subject. My mama insistently says, "You can rest when I die knowing you have taken good care of me." How the sweetest words can simultaneously cause me to shed tears of joy and pain should be obvious. I strive to take good care of my mother and to see her happy, but I also know God's best for my mother can't and won't be manifested on earth, but eternally in God's presence one day. Every daughter reading this devotion would do good to take good care of their mother.

Let Us Pray: Heavenly Father, for as long as I have my mother here on earth with me, help me to do all I can for as long as I can, to express my love and appreciation for all she has done for me. I pray I can brighten her days, lighten her load, and bring joy to her heart. Bless me with more than enough so that I can supply my daily needs and relieve my mother of her daily needs as well. As you bless me, I thank you for helping me to bless her. In Jesus's name I pray. Amen.

Let Us Learn the Spiritual Lesson: John 19:25–27 (NIV) "Near the cross of Jesus stood his mother, his mother's sister, Mary the wife of Cleopas, and Mary Magdalene. When Jesus saw his mother there, and the disciple whom he loved standing nearby, he said to her, 'Woman, here is your son,' and to the disciple, 'Here is your mother.' From that time on, this disciple took her into his home."

Let Us Reflect: What have you learned? What can you do better or differently now?

_____
_____
_____
_____
_____
_____
_____

Upcoming Books

1. *Flourishing in the Famine: The Right Appetite Matters, an In-Depth Look at the Fruit of the Spirit*
2. *Spiritually Dressed for Success: The Right Attitude Matters, an In-Depth Look at the Beatitudes*
3. *The Beauty, Blessing, and Burden of Preaching: A Woman's Biblical Perspective*

Contact Info:
www.ccreations.org
P O Box 35905
Houston, Texas 77235-5905
Telephone: 832.528.2371
Email:yolandaburroughs@ccreations.org

Follower Her:
Facebook/Youtube/Instagram@Yolandaburroughs
Twitter @yolandaburrough

A woman when she is in travail hath sorrow, because her hour is come: but as soon as she is delivered of the child, she remembereth no more the anguish, for joy that a man is born into the world.
—John 16:21 (KJV)

Nothing is more beautiful than the bond a mother shares with her daughter, and a godly mother joyfully loving and raising her. With thoughtful prayers to God, wise words, practical instructions, and firm discipline, she teaches everyday principles that will surely bless the daughter who hears and obeys. This devotional will help daughters understand the words Mama say and enhance mother-daughter communication with God and each other. After all, God gave the gift of mother and daughter, and a good relationship is the gift mother and daughter can give back to God. This devotional will help you celebrate and cultivate the gift!

Children are a heritage from the LORD; offspring a reward from him.
—Psalm 127:3 (NIV)

Made in the USA
Coppell, TX
12 May 2022